THE MAN WHO
PLANTED TREES

JEAN GIONO was born in 1895 in Manosque, Provence, and lived there most of his life. He supported his family working as a bank clerk for eighteen years before his first two novels were published, thanks to the generosity of André Gide, to critical acclaim. He went on to write thirty novels, including *The Horseman on the Roof*, and numerous essays and stories. In 1953, the year in which he wrote *The Man who Planted Trees*, he was awarded the Prix Monégasque for his collective work. Jean Giono died in October 1970.

THE MAN WHO PLANTED TREES

JEAN GIONO

Translated by Barbara Bray
with an Afterword by Aline Giono
Wood engravings by Harry Brockway

THE HARVILL PRESS
LONDON

This edition first published in 1995 by
The Harvill Press
84 Thornhill Road
London N1 1RD

3 5 7 9 8 6 4

Afterword copyright © Aline Giono, 1975
L'Homme qui Plantait des Arbres
copyright © Éditions Gallimard, 1980
English translation copyright © Barbara Bray, 1995
Wood engravings copyright © Harry Brockway, 1995

A CIP catalogue record for this title is
available from the British Library

ISBN 1 86046 117 4

Designed and typeset by
Libanus Press, Marlborough, Wilts

Printed and bound in Great Britain by Butler & Tanner Ltd
at Selwood Printing, Burgess Hill

To see a human being reveal really exceptional qualities one must be able to observe his activities over many years. If these activities are completely unselfish; if the idea motivating them is unique in its magnanimity; if it is quite certain they have never looked for any reward; and if in addition they have left visible traces on the world — then one may say, without fear of error, that one is in the presence of an unforgettable character.

About forty years ago I went on a long journey, on foot, through the uplands, utterly unknown to tourists, of the ancient region where the Alps extend into Provence.

The area is bounded in the south-east and the south by the middle reaches of the river Durance, between Sisteron and Mirabeau; in the north by the upper course of the Drôme, from its source down as far as Die; and in the west by the plains of the Comtat Venaissin and the foothills of Mont Ventoux. It includes all the northern part of the department of the Basses-Alpes, the south of the Drôme, and a small enclave of the Vaucluse.

When I went on my long tramp through that deserted region, between 1200 and 1300 metres above sea level, it was an expanse of bare and monotonous moorland. All that grew there was wild lavender.

I set out to cross the area at its widest point, and after walking for three days found myself in a landscape of unparalleled desolation. I camped near the skeleton of a deserted village. I hadn't had any water since the previous day, and I had to find some. Although the houses, huddled together there like an old wasps' nest, were in ruins, they made me think there must once have been a spring or a well nearby. And indeed there was a spring, but it had dried up. The five or six roofless houses weathered away by the wind and the rain, and the little chapel with its fallen tower, were arranged like the houses and churches in living villages. But in them no life remained.

It was a fine day in June, very sunny, but on those bare heights, open to the sky, the wind blew cruelly. The sound of it raging through the carcasses of the houses was like the snarl of a wild beast disturbed over its prey.

I had to move on. But after walking for five hours I still hadn't found water, and there was nothing to suggest I was going to. Everywhere the same dry land, the same tough grass. Then I thought I could see a little black figure standing upright in the distance. I took it for the trunk of a solitary tree. But on the off chance I set out towards it. It was a shepherd. Thirty or so sheep lay resting on the baking earth nearby. He gave me a drink from his flask, and then, a little while later, took me to his fold, which was hidden in a hollow. He got his water, which was delicious, from a very deep natural well, over which he had rigged up a rudimentary windlass.

He said very little. This is common in people who live alone, but you could tell he was sure of himself and confident in his self-possession, which was surprising in such a dismal spot. The place he lived in was not just a hut but a real house built of stone: you could see where he'd patched up the ruin it must have been before. The roof was strong and kept out the rain. The wind in the tiles made a sound like the sea on the shore.

Inside, the house was tidy, the washing-up done, the floor swept, the shepherd's gun cleaned and oiled. His soup was cooking over the fire. I noticed now that he was freshly shaved, that all his buttons were sewn on firmly, and that his clothes were mended with such minute care the repairs were almost invisible.

He insisted I should share his soup, and afterwards, when I offered him my tobacco pouch, he said he didn't smoke. His dog, as silent as he, was friendly without fawning.

It had been agreed from the outset that I'd spend the night there: the nearest village was still more than a day and a half's walk away. Moreover, I knew what they were like, the rare villages one did come across in that part of the world. There were four or five of them sparsely scattered over these slopes, buried in thickets of holm oak where usable roads petered out.

The villages are inhabited by charcoal burners. Life is hard there. Families, crowded together in a climate

as harsh in summer as in winter, seethe with conflicting egoisms. Ambitions swell to wild proportions among them, so desperate and unrelenting is the desire to escape.

The men drive their vans into town with their charcoal, and then drive back again. Even the stoutest character goes to pieces under the continual contrast. The women stay at home and nurse grudges. Everything is a subject of unrelenting contention and rivalry, from the selling of charcoal to a pew in church, from separate and competing vices to the general mixture of vice and virtue. Never any rest. And on top of all that, the equally unrelenting wind frays everyone's nerves. There are epidemics of suicide and many cases of madness, usually homicidal.

The shepherd who didn't smoke went and fetched a little bag and emptied a pile of acorns on to the table. Then he began to inspect them closely, separating the good from the bad. I smoked my pipe. I offered to help. He said he had to do it himself. And seeing how carefully he worked I didn't insist. That was all the conversation we had. And when he'd collected a large enough heap of good acorns he divided them up into groups of ten. As he did so he discarded those that were too small or had a tiny split; he examined them minutely. Once he had sorted out one hundred perfect acorns, he stopped and we went to bed.

It was peaceful to be in his company, and next morning I asked if I might stay all day and rest. He found this quite natural; or rather he gave me the impression that nothing disturbed him. I didn't absolutely need to rest, but I was intrigued and wanted to know more. He let his flock out of the fold and led them to pasture. Before leaving home he took the little bag in which he'd put his carefully chosen and counted acorns, and dipped it in a bucket of water.

I noticed that instead of a stick he carried a steel rod as thick as a man's thumb and about a metre and a half long. I followed a path parallel to his, strolling along like someone taking it easy. He took his sheep to a hollow and left them there to

graze, guarded by his dog. Then he came up to where I was standing. I was afraid he was going to object to my intrusion, but not at all. He had to come this way anyhow, and he invited me to go with him if I hadn't anything better to do.

When he reached the place he was aiming for, he began making holes in the ground with his rod, putting an acorn in each and then covering it up again. He was planting oak trees. I asked him if the land was his. He said it wasn't. Did he know who the owner was? No, he didn't. He thought it must be common land, or perhaps it belonged to people who weren't interested in it. He wasn't interested in who they were. And so, with great care, he planted his hundred acorns.

After the midday meal he started sorting out more acorns to sow. I must have been very pressing with my questions, because he answered them. He'd been planting trees in this wilderness for three years. He'd planted a hundred thousand of them. Out of those, twenty thousand had come up. Of the twenty thousand he expected to lose half, because of rodents or the unpredictable ways of Providence. That still meant ten thousand oaks would grow where before there had been nothing.

It was at this point that I wondered how old he was. He was obviously over fifty. Fifty-five, he said. His name was Elzéard Bouffier. He had once owned a farm on the plains. It was there he had lived his life.

But he had lost first his only son, then his wife. After that he came here to be alone, enjoying an unhurried existence with his sheep and his dog. But it struck him that this part of the country was dying for lack of trees, and having nothing much else to do he decided to put things right.

As I myself, despite my youth, was leading a solitary life at the time, I was able to sympathise with others like me and deal tactfully with their sensibilities. But I made one mistake with him. Because I was young I naturally thought of the future in terms of myself, and assumed everyone sought the same happiness. So I remarked how magnificent his ten

thousand oak trees would be in thirty years' time. He answered quite simply that, if God spared him, he'd have planted so many other trees in those thirty years, the ten thousand would be just a drop in the ocean.

He was already studying the reproduction of beeches, and close to the house was a nursery of saplings grown from beechnuts. He'd put up a fence to protect them from the sheep, and they were already fine specimens. He was also thinking of birches for low-lying spots, where according to him there was a certain amount of humidity a few metres below the surface.

We parted the following morning.

The year after that the 1914 war broke out, and I was in the army for five years. As an infantryman I hadn't much time to think about trees. And to tell the truth, the episode hadn't affected me all that much: I thought of the oaks as a hobby, like stamp collecting. So I forgot about them.

When the 1914 war was over I found myself with a small amount of demob money and a great desire to breathe some fresh air. So with no other purpose but that I set out again for the same deserted landscapes as before.

The country itself hadn't changed. But when I got beyond the dead village I could see in the distance a kind of grey mist covering the hills like a carpet. Since the previous evening I'd started thinking about the tree-planting shepherd again. "Ten thousand oaks take up a lot of room," I reflected.

I'd seen so many people die in the last five years I could easily imagine that Elzéard Bouffier must be dead too. The more so as, when you're twenty, men of fifty seem like old codgers with one foot in the grave. But he wasn't dead. On the contrary, he was still very spry. He had adopted a different calling. There were only four ewes left, but now he had about a hundred beehives. He'd got rid of the sheep because they were a threat to his trees. For, as he told me, and as I could see for myself, he had taken no notice of the war and gone on imperturbably planting trees.

By this time the 1910 oaks were ten years old and taller than both him and me. They were an impressive sight. I was left literally speechless, and as he didn't speak either we spent the whole day walking silently through his forest. It was in three sections, and measured eleven kilometres across at its widest point. When you remembered that it had all emerged from the hands and spirit of this one man, without any technical aids, you saw that men could be as efficient as God in other things beside destruction.

He'd stuck to all his plans, as was evident from the beech trees that came up to my shoulder and stretched away as far as the eye could see. The oaks were thick and dense, and past the age of being at the mercy of rodents. As for Providence and its powers of destruction, it would have taken a hurricane now to undo the shepherd's creation. He showed me some beautiful birch plantations dating from five years back — 1915, when I was fighting at Verdun. He'd put them in all the

low-lying places, where he had rightly suspected there was dampness just beneath the surface of the soil. They were as fresh and tender as youths, and full of the will to live.

There seemed to be a sort of chain reaction in all this creation, but Elzéard Bouffier didn't trouble about that: he just went stubbornly on with his task, simple and natural as ever. But going back down through the village I saw there was water flowing in streams that had been dry as long as anyone could remember. As chain reactions go, this was the most remarkable one I'd ever seen. The last time those brooks had flowed was in very ancient times.

Some of the dreary villages I mentioned at the beginning of this story were built on the sites of old Gallo-Roman villages, of which some traces still remained. Archaeologists had dug up fish hooks where, in the twentieth century, storage tanks were the only source of water.

Seeds were carried on the wind, too, so as the

water reappeared, so did willows, reeds, meadows, gardens, flowers and some reason for living.

But the change came about so slowly, people got used to it and took it for granted. Hunters coming up into lonely places after hares and wild boar had noticed lots of young saplings, but they put it down to the whim of nature. That was why no one interfered with what the shepherd had done. If they'd suspected what he was up to they'd have tried to stop him. But no one did suspect it. How could anyone, whether in the villages or in government offices, have imagined such perseverance, such magnificent generosity?

From 1920 on, I never let a year go by without paying Elzéard Bouffier a visit. I never saw him weaken or doubt. And yet God knows God Himself gave him cause to! I never counted up the setbacks and disappointments he met with. But inevitably so great an achievement must have had to surmount some adversity, and such a passion couldn't have won through without some struggles against despair. He spent a year planting over ten thousand maples.

They all died. The following year he dropped maples and went back to beeches, which turned out to be even more of a success than the oaks.

One cannot properly appreciate this rare character unless one remembers that he accomplished what he did in complete solitude. So complete was his isolation that towards the end of his life he got out of the habit of speaking. Or did he no longer see any need for speech?

In 1933 he had a visit from a shocked forest warden who told him he mustn't light fires out of doors in case he endangered the "natural" forest.

This was the first time ever, replied the simple shepherd, that a forest had sprung up of its own accord. By this time he'd taken to going and planting beech trees twelve kilometres away from where he lived. To save himself having to go home every night — he was seventy-five by now — he decided he would build a stone hut among the young trees. He built it the following year.

In 1935 a government delegation came to inspect the "natural forest". The visitors included a senior official from the Forestry Commission, a member of parliament and several technicians. There was much empty talk. It was decided that something must be done, but fortunately nothing "was" done. Except for one useful measure: the forest was placed under the protection of the State, and charcoal burning was forbidden there. For it was impossible not to be overwhelmed by the beauty of those young and healthy trees. Even the member of parliament was entranced.

One of the senior forest wardens in the delegation was a friend of mine. I explained the mystery to him, and one day during the following week we set out together to see Elzéard Bouffier. We found him hard at work twenty kilometres away from where the delegation had carried out their inspection. The senior warden wasn't my friend for nothing: he knew what was what, and didn't say anything. I handed over a few eggs that I'd brought as a present, and we divided our provisions into three. As we ate, and for some time after, we just

gazed silently at the landscape. In the direction we'd come from the land was covered with trees between six and seven metres high. I recalled what it looked like in 1913: a wilderness.

Peaceful and regular work, a frugal way of life, the bracing air of the uplands, and above all his tranquillity of mind — all these had given the old man an almost awesome good health. He was an athlete of God. I wondered how many more hectares he was going to cover with trees. Before we left, my friend briefly and simply suggested that certain other trees might be very suitable for this terrain, though he didn't press the point. "After all, he's wiser than I am," he said. Then, after my friend and I had walked on for about an hour, he added: "He's the wisest man in the world! He's discovered a perfect recipe for happiness!"

Because of my friend, not only the forest but also our hero's happiness was protected: three subordinates were appointed, and bullied to such good purpose that they remained unmoved by any bribes the woodcutters might tempt them with.

The tree-planter's work wasn't really threatened until the 1939 war. In those days cars were run on machines that turned wood into gas, and there was never enough wood. People started cutting down the oaks that had been planted in 1910, but the trees were so far from main roads that the business didn't pay and was abandoned. The shepherd didn't even know about it. He was thirty kilometres away, going peacefully on with his task, ignoring the 1939 war just as he'd ignored the war of 1914.

I saw Elzéard Bouffier for the last time in June 1945. He was then eighty-seven. I took the same route into the wilds as before, but now, although everything had been allowed to run down during the war, there was a bus service linking the valley of the Durance and the mountains. I assumed it was because I was driving through the country relatively fast that I didn't recognise scenery I'd seen for the first time on foot. Some of the settlements we went through also seemed quite new. It was only when I found out the names of the villages that I knew I really was back in a region that had once been ruined and desolate. The bus set me down in Vergons.

In 1913 this hamlet, with its ten or eleven houses, had had three inhabitants. They were rough, unsociable people who hated one another and lived by trapping animals, in a state that morally and physically was almost prehistoric. The empty houses around them were overrun by nettles. They lived with nothing to hope for; all they had to look forward to was death. Not a situation propitious to virtue.

But now all was changed, even the air. Instead of the rough and arid gusts that I had met with before, there was a soft and scented breeze. A sound like water drifted down from the heights: it was the wind in the forests. But the most astonishing thing of all was the sound of water actually flowing into a basin. I saw that the people in the village had built a fountain: it was gushing forth in abundance, and — this was what moved me most — beside it they had planted a lime tree which must have been about four years old. It was already quite sturdy — an indisputable symbol of resurrection.

Vergons showed others signs of work that's not undertaken without hope. So hope had returned.

The ruins had been tidied up, crumbling walls knocked down, and five old houses rebuilt. The hamlet now had twenty-eight inhabitants, including four young couples. The new houses were freshly roughcast and surrounded by kitchen gardens where rows of both vegetables and flowers grew: cabbages mingled with rose bushes, leeks with snapdragons, celery with anemones. It had become a place where one would wish to live.

I continued on foot. The war was only just over and life was still restricted, but Lazarus had risen from the grave. On the lower slopes of the mountains I could see small fields of young barley and rye, and, deep in the narrow valleys, a green haze of meadows.

In the eight years between then and now the whole region has grown healthy and prosperous. On the sites where I saw only ruins in 1913 there are now neat, well-plastered farmhouses that speak of a

happy and comfortable existence. Ancient springs, fed by the rains and snows retained by the forests, have started flowing again, and the water from them has been carefully channelled. Near every farm, amid groves of maple, the basins of fountains overflow on to carpets of cool mint. Villages have been gradually rebuilt. People from the plains, where land is expensive, have come and settled here, bringing with them youth and movement and the spirit of adventure. Along the lanes and paths you meet men and women who are well-fed, boys and girls who know how to laugh and have rediscovered the pleasures of old rural sports and pastimes. If you include both the former population, unrecognisable since their life became more agreeable, and the newcomers, more than ten thousand people must owe their happiness to Elzéard Bouffier.

When I reflect on the fact that one man, with only his own simple physical and moral resources, was able to bring forth out of the desert this land of Canaan, I can't help feeling the human condition in general is admirable, in spite of everything. And when I count up all the constancy, magnanimity, perseverance and generosity it took to achieve those results, I'm filled with enormous respect for the old, uneducated peasant who was able, unaided, to carry through to a successful conclusion an achievement worthy of God.

Elzéard Bouffier died peacefully in 1947 in the hospice at Banon.

THE STORY OF
ELZEARD BOUFFIER

ALINE GIONO

My father's story, which you've just read, has had several titles:

The Man who Planted Trees;
The Story of Elzéard Bouffier;
The Man who Planted Hope and Reaped Happiness.

Also "The Most Extraordinary Character I Ever Met"; and perhaps others I know nothing about. Until now the story has appeared only in reviews, newspapers and magazines, usually abroad (it has been translated into twelve different languages) and in the most varied countries. As we have seen, its title has varied too. But what hasn't changed is the welcome the story has met with, as is shown by a continual flood of enthusiastic letters. But it hasn't always been so: the tale has had a curious history. I'll start at the beginning.

In 1953 the American magazine *Reader's Digest* asked my father to write a few pages for its well-known feature, "The Most Extraordinary Character I Ever Met".

My father loved commissions. He was never happier

than when someone asked him to write so many words on such and such a subject; if they actually specified the number of words he was in seventh heaven. If he'd been commissioned to produce 3,400 words on shoe-laces, he'd have set about the task with glee. (One illustration of this, among others, is "Stones", a text he wrote on the subject of precious stones, a commission from a factory producing jewels for Swiss watches.)

But he objected strongly to some kinds of commission. Long before the war he'd done some interviews with politicians. "Those people would ask you to write a novel about sewing machines!" he said angrily, going on to provide brilliant examples of how such a commission might be executed. He was indignant because it treated writing as something other than craftsmanship pure and simple.

To return to *Reader's Digest*, I can still see my father going cheerfully up to his study and starting work.

A few days later the text, typed by my mother, was sent off, and the response wasn't slow in coming.

It expressed the warmest satisfaction: the piece was exactly what was wanted.

A few more weeks went by, and one fine day my father, looking very astonished, hurried down from his study, through the dining room, and out to join my mother in the kitchen. He'd just had another letter from *Reader's Digest*, very different in tone from the first. It called my father an impostor, and with a great show of virtuous indignation was returning his text: the *Digest* couldn't publish it.

This is what had happened. *Reader's Digest*, being a serious magazine, subjected its contributors' texts to thorough investigation. The public must not be misled: if the most remarkable mother was said to have had twenty-four children in twelve years, her claim had to be checked out. If the most remarkable missionary was supposed to have been cut up into seventy-four pieces before he was eaten . . . And so on. In short, it had to be established that every extraordinary person had had a life that was ordinary, i.e. real.

The remarkable person my father had described was a shepherd. In 1953 this hadn't yet come back into fashion. What made him remarkable was that he'd spent his life — all his life — planting acorns wherever he went with his flock. So gradually, thanks to him, an almost deserted area was magnificently re-wooded and restored to life and abundance. It was a charming fable, and its hero was reminiscent of the Americans' Johnny Appleseed or the John Barleycorn of the English.

My father, giving him life, just as Elzéard Bouffier himself gave life back to the wilderness, was imprudent enough to plant in his narrative not acorns but a few easily verifiable geographical details, and then had his hero die (peacefully) in the hospice at Banon in 1947.

The idea that someone should seriously check whether someone called Elzéard Bouffier — what a beautiful name! — died in the hospice at Banon in 1947 would have struck my father as farcical. But that is what happened.

Of course the researcher drew a blank. There was no Elzéard at Banon, no enchanted forest at Vergons in the Var. In short, it was all an obvious fake. Hence the outrage.

My father found the situation comical, but, as I well remember, his chief reaction was surprise that there should be people stupid enough to ask a writer — a professional inventor — who was the most remarkable person he had ever met, and not realise that this person was bound to emerge from his imagination.

It was a family joke for a long time.

But after being buried a second time by *Reader's Digest*, Elzéard Bouffier has had a posthumous existence as remarkable as his imaginary real life.

He has gone and planted his acorns and grown his forests all over the world, from New Zealand to Kenya, from Finland to the United States. Wherever his story has been published, people have believed in it; though this simply proves it was well told. But why shouldn't people believe in it? Nature imitates art, and it wouldn't surprise me if someone actually found an elderly shepherd who'd spent his life reforesting whole landscapes. In fact, I'm sure he does exist. But maybe he hasn't got such a fine name.

I hope what I'm about to relate won't shock people with no sense of humour. I've come across a correspondence that took place in 1968 between my father and a German publishing house. I don't know by what mysterious chance this German publisher, who planned to bring out an anthology of illustrated biographies, decided to include the life of Elzéard Bouffier. But the fact is, the invented shepherd was going to appear among real people, historical personages, or at least characters who had actually existed — a list of their names was enclosed. And so a photograph was required, and my father was solemnly requested to send one.

I can still see my father laughing. It was hard to resist such an opportunity for a joke. The letter from Germany is annotated in his handwriting:

"I sent them a photograph of the *invented* character" (his italics). With the letter, in a plastic sleeve, scrupulously returned by the German publisher with many thanks, there's a little old faded photograph of a typical "handsome old man", clear-eyed and with a calm expression, his bearing both proud and awkward, wearing what is clearly his Sunday best in honour of the occasion. Elzéard Bouffier, as large as life and twice as natural! The name is written on the back of the photograph in my father's hand. And so this unknown stranger will for ever be Elzéard Bouffier — unless someone recognises him, and we get a letter claiming compensation for wrongful exploitation of their grandfather.

The German publisher's last letter is dated 1969. The anthology of biographies was such a success it had gone into a third edition. And "many of our readers are so enthusiastic they would like to go to France to see the places where Elzéard Bouffier lived and planted the forest. We should be very grateful if you would be so kind as to send us the exact address of the village which is closest to the forest, and also the nearest railway station."

What better tribute could one offer any writer?

I don't know whether my father went so far as to invent a railway station to please his German readers, for sadly all this happened in 1969, and the next year he was to stop inventing for ever.